Tomatoes for Neela

by **Padma Lakshmi**

illustrated by
Juana Martinez-Neal

VIKING

Neela loved cooking with her amma in their cozy kitchen. There was a lovely portrait of her paati that hung over them, watching them cook.

hummus

roasted cauliflower

mashed potatoes

spaghetti and meatballs

chipotle aioli

ramen

rice pilaf

spicy lentil stew

chimichurri

roasted chicken

steak and fries

dosas

ceviche

mango pudding

passion fruit cheesecake

sushi

Neela and her amma made all kinds of yummy recipes. There were cakes and puddings, and sauces always bubbling away.

dumplings

flan

lemon loaf

pesto

French omelet

saffron rice

Tomato Sauce

10 plum tomatoes
1/4 cup olive oil
5-6 med. cloves garlic
2-3 bay leaves
salt
pepper
1/4 - 1/2 tsp. sugar

3. Water boiling lower
tomato (carefully) let
for 3 minutes. Remove
each tomato

4. Peel tomatoes. Cut

5. Skillet, Add oil, gently
over low heat. Add garlic
Cover. Lower heat.

6. Add tomatoes and
Sauce. Medium low

7. Add some if needed

Amma scribbled all their recipes into a big notebook. It was always open. Neela loved to sit on the counter and copy the recipes into her own notebook, too. Among the spices and nuts, there sat another cloth-covered book on the shelf. This one looked old and important, like it was full of spells and belonged to a wizard. But it had actually once belonged to her paati, and one day, it would belong to Neela.

Saturday was Neela's favorite day of the week. They were going to the green market!

The market was always buzzing with customers and now brimming with crops from the end of summer. Juicy ripe peaches, plump blueberries, golden corn topped with stringy silk so shiny, it looked like the hair on Neela's doll. The best time of the year!

And best of all: tomatoes!

Neela smiled at the heirloom tomatoes with their funny shapes and ridges. Amma explained, "They are called 'heirlooms' because their seeds are passed down from season to season. So they always maintain their deep flavor." These tomatoes reminded Neela of Paati's cookbook.

Neela and Amma brought back a bag bursting with plump, juicy plum tomatoes. Plum tomatoes were the best for making her paati's favorite tomato sauce because they had fewer seeds. Making sauce was something she had done at the end of every summer, right before school started, since Neela could remember.

Neela loved how the sauce tasted, but the sweetest part was that it made her feel closer to her paati, who lived far away in India. Neela unpacked their treasure onto the counter as she smiled up at her paati's portrait.

Neela always helped her amma. She shelled peas in the spring, peeled sweet potatoes in the fall, and even sprinkled and stirred spices into dishes. Neela loved listening to her amma tell stories while they cooked together. Many of these tales had been passed down from mothers to their daughters.

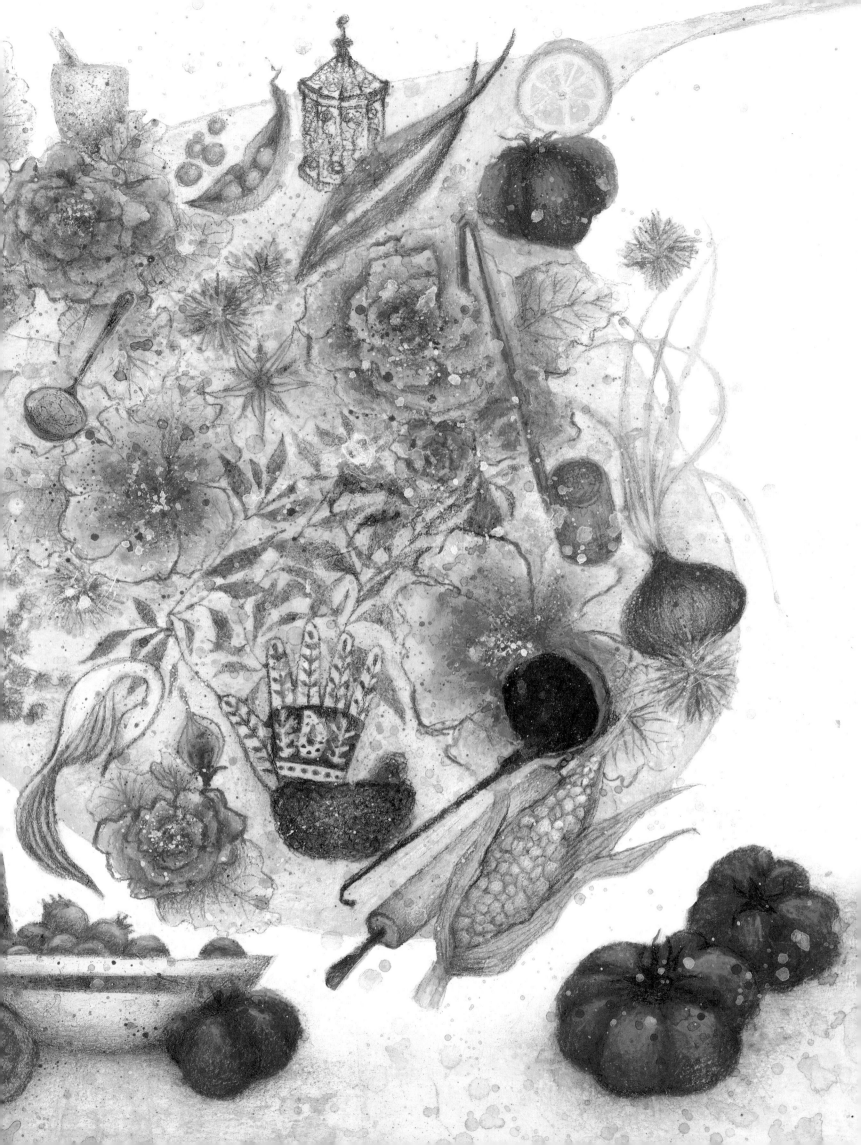

Amma washed and carefully cut Xs on the bottom of each tomato. Then she dropped them in boiling water for just a few minutes. After she strained them and they were cool enough to touch, Neela began to peel them.

Next, Amma cut them over a bowl, saving the juices and seeds. Neela peeled garlic. And then Amma sliced and fried the garlic gently with oil in the pan.

At times, Amma moved so quickly, the bangles on her wrists made pretty clinking sounds. This was music to Neela's ears. There was a slow rhythm when she chopped, faster beats when she shook spices. But the loudest, and most fun, was when her amma shredded carrots with the box grater!

When the garlic was just barely golden, Amma added the tomatoes to the pan. Neela shook in the salt and Amma stirred, her bangles clicking and clacking. Neela danced around to the rhythm of the bracelets' music. Then she dropped in a few bay leaves so that Amma could stir again.

Amma put a lid on the pan and showed Neela how to carefully lower the flame, just so. The sauce simmered. The room smelled deliciously of warm tomatoes and roasted garlic.

MEXICO

tomatl

THE AMERICAS

PERU

tomato

"Did you know that 'tomato' comes from an old Aztec word, 'tomatl'? They traveled from the New World all the way to Europe and even India long ago," Amma said. "People thought tomatoes were pretty but feared they were poisonous!"

Neela laughed at the idea of being afraid of a tomato.

tomate

EVrope

Ṭamétā
टमेटो

tamaatar
टमाटर

takkāḷi
தக்காளி

"Over the years, people in Spain and Italy began to cook them in sauces and stews and found they were just delicious!"

omodoro

INDIA

Neela wrote these notes
down in her recipe book in
clear letters. She was excited
to show her paati what she
had learned about tomatoes
and how she could make the
family tomato sauce when
she would come to visit in
the winter.

"Sauce is ready. Want a taste?"
Amma asked.
"Yes!" Neela said.

She ate slowly, letting the warm sauce
coat her mouth. This was the taste
they would savor all winter, when the
air grew cold and tomatoes were no
longer in season.

"But why can't we just buy tomatoes then, Amma?"

"Because tomatoes grow on vines on the longest days of the year, when it's hot enough to go swimming. They need to swim in the sun." Amma explained that tomatoes picked when in season not only taste better; they are better for you.

"It's best to have fruits and vegetables when Mother Nature likes to grow them near us," Amma said.

All Neela knew was that cooking tomatoes in summer would make her happy in the winter, too. Made into simple pasta sauce or yummy chutney, used to stew beans for chili, or turned into salsa for enchiladas—the tomatoes would fill containers and canned jars that would be the pride and joy of their kitchen.

Now they just had to save enough to have tomatoes in the winter.

Neela placed a special jar of tomato sauce in the back of the cupboard that she would save for Paati's next visit. That way, she could be a part of this special Saturday, too. One day soon, they would share these sweet flavors together.

PAATI'S TOMATO SAUCE

This is a super-simple recipe that is delicious served over pasta, drizzled over eggs, or used as a sauce for pizza. It also freezes well.

2 ½ pounds or 10 plum tomatoes
¼ cup olive oil
5–6 medium cloves of garlic, peeled and sliced lengthwise into thirds
2–3 medium bay leaves, preferably fresh
kosher salt to taste (approximately 1 teaspoon)
crushed black pepper and/or red pepper flakes to taste
¼–½ teaspoon sugar (only if not using peak-season tomatoes)

Ask an adult for help with this recipe.

1. Set a large pot of water to boil.

2. With a knife, carefully cut an X on the smooth bottom end of each tomato (the bottom is the end without the stem). Each line should measure ¾ inches long. (This can be done with a serrated butter knife instead of a sharp knife, for safety.)

3. When the water is vigorously boiling, carefully lower each tomato into the pot with a slotted spoon. Fully immerse all the tomatoes in the boiling water. Let the tomatoes boil 3 minutes or until you see the Xs get wider and pull open slightly. Use the slotted spoon to remove each tomato. Let the tomatoes cool enough to touch.

4. Peel back each corner of the skin, all the way to the other end of the tomato. Repeat for each tomato. If it's difficult to peel the skin, simply immerse the tomato back into the boiling water for a minute or two. Cut any remaining peel and stem end off the tomato. Cut each tomato into 8 pieces, reserving as much juice as you can.

5. In a deep skillet, an adult should heat the oil on medium to medium-low, depending on your stove. Add the slices of garlic. Stir to coat the garlic with oil and cover the pan, checking every 3 minutes and stirring. Covering the pan will help soften the garlic as it fries. Lower the heat if it sizzles too hard, because you want the garlic to be just barely tinged golden yellow, not browned. You don't want it to burn on the outside and still be raw on the inside either! You can tilt the pan up so that all the oil pools and garlic is immersed in oil for a few minutes, thus cooking it evenly. Do not let the garlic cook too quickly. It should take 5–7 minutes to cook, but you can lower the flame and cook it a bit longer to ensure it cooks properly. Taking longer to cook the garlic on lower heat will ensure a better flavor, reducing the chance of bitterness that comes from overcooking or burning garlic.

6. Slowly add the tomatoes to the skillet, being careful not to splatter. Add the bay leaves and a sprinkle of salt, and stir. Cover the skillet. Keep the heat at medium-low. Check the sauce every 5 minutes. Lift the lid, let the water on the underside of the lid pour back into the pan, and stir well. Repeat this for 20–25 more minutes, until the sauce darkens. Taste and add additional salt if needed, as well as red and black pepper to taste. (For younger kids, use just a smidge of black pepper.)

7. If the sauce tastes too sour, add some sugar, pinch by pinch. Stir. Let the tomatoes cook uncovered for another 15 minutes, stirring every 5 minutes. Let cool and divide into freezer-safe glass containers or use immediately for pasta or pizza (for pizza sauce, add 1 teaspoon of oregano when first adding salt). Makes 2 cups.

NEELA's TOMATO CHUTNEY

This simple chutney gives a zing to any meal. Use it like ketchup or a mild hot sauce. It's great with eggs and toast, on a hot dog, or spread onto a grilled cheese sandwich before heating (or to dip in after). Use with tortilla chips in place of salsa, or to make nachos. Use it in a quesadilla. Serve with rice pilaf. Stir it into hot plain rice with ghee or a pat of butter. Spoon it over grilled chicken, fish, or steak.

This chutney is also a great base for a gravied curry with mixed vegetables, pulses, lentils, or any meat. Just add some good curry powder like garam masala or Madras sambar powder but reduce the simmering time by several minutes so it's looser and more sauce-like. The possibilities are endless.

PEPPER

SALT

CANOLA OIL

CUMIN SEED

MUSTARD SEED

¼ cup canola oil
1 teaspoon cumin seeds
½ teaspoon brown or black mustard seeds
1 cup yellow onion, diced
2 tablespoons minced garlic (about 3 large cloves)
2 tablespoons peeled, minced ginger (2-inch piece)
2 dozen fresh curry leaves, torn into rough bits (optional)
¼ teaspoon ground turmeric
¼ teaspoon cayenne, or to taste
2 pounds tomatoes, roughly chopped
1 teaspoon sugar (optional)
kosher salt and black pepper to taste

TOMATOES

ONION

GARLIC

GINGER

CURRY LEAF

TURMERIC

CAYENNE

Ask an adult for help with this recipe.

1. Heat the oil in a deep skillet on medium heat. When hot, lower the heat slightly and add the cumin and mustard seeds. Sauté. Be careful, as the mustard seeds will pop out of the pan when they get hot!

2. When the mustard seeds start popping, quickly add the onion, garlic, and ginger. Stir often and sauté until the onions are glassy, about 5–7 minutes. Now add the curry leaves (if you choose), turmeric, and cayenne. Cook together for another 2–3 minutes, mixing well.

3. Add the tomatoes in carefully and stir well. Once the tomatoes start to break down (6–8 minutes), add ½ cup water and salt to taste (about 1 teaspoon) and stir. Cover and lower the heat to a simmer. Let it cook, stirring often, for 10–15 minutes. Remove the cover and cook for another 15 minutes, stirring occasionally. Stir in a bit more water if it sticks, 1–2 tablespoons at a time. You want a loose, jammy consistency at the end. Taste it. Does it need anything?

4. Now it should be tangy. Adjust salt or add sugar only if needed, one pinch at a time. Add black pepper and additional cayenne to taste. Remove from heat and let cool. Store in a tight glass container or jar in the fridge for up to 3–4 days. Makes 2 cups.

Tomato Fun Facts

Tomatoes are a fruit and not a vegetable. This is because they have seeds and grow from a flowering plant.

There are around ten thousand varieties of tomatoes!

Tomatoes come in many colors: red, yellow, orange, pink, purple, black, and white.

Tomatoes originated in the Andes Mountains of what are now Peru, Chile, Bolivia, and Ecuador and were first used by the Aztecs in Mesoamerica as food.

Tomatoes were first brought to Europe in the 1500s.

China produces the most tomatoes, followed by the United States and India.

Tomatoes are rich in a healthy antioxidant called lycopene.

The original Aztec name for tomato, "tomatl," translates to "plump thing with navel." The Italian word for tomato, "pomodoro," translates to "golden apple."

The scientific name for the tomato is *Solanum lycopersicum*, which means "wolf peach."

Tomato season is typically in summer and early fall. In the United States, most tomatoes are grown in California (year-round) and Florida (October through June).

About Farmworkers

Tomatoes for Neela is about the importance of connecting with family, tradition, and culture through food. But it's also about honoring the food we eat and the many people who help bring it to us. The tomatoes you eat have been on a journey to get to you. Before they arrived at your supermarket, green market, or restaurant, they were picked, carried, and loaded onto trucks by farmworkers. They have hard jobs to do: they work long hours in the sun, they lift and carry heavy buckets of tomatoes and other produce, and they are often exposed to harsh chemicals called pesticides that help grow large amounts of fruits and vegetables. Many farmworkers travel to the United States from Central and South America to find work to support their families. They accept low pay and work under difficult conditions because they do not have the protections of a work visa or of being a US citizen. Farmworkers are afraid that they will be deported and forced to leave the United States, so instead, they endure unfair treatment.

Civil rights activists, like César Chávez, Dolores Huerta, and so many others spend their lives fighting for the dignity and basic rights of farmworkers, and thanks to them, we now have organizations like the Fair Food Program (fairfoodprogram.org), the United Farm Workers (ufw.org), Farmworker Justice (farmworkerjustice.org), the Coalition of Immokalee Workers (ciw-online.org), and the Dolores Huerta Foundation (doloreshuerta.org). They work to help migrant and seasonal farmworkers to improve their working conditions, understand their rights and protections, and further immigration reform. It's important that we keep our Earth, our food, and our farmworkers safe.

For more information, please explore the resources above and these books for kids:

A Picture Book of Cesar Chavez by David A. Adler and Michael S. Adler, illustrated by Marie Olofsdotter
Side by Side/Lado a Lado: The Story of Dolores Huerta and César Chávez/La Historia de Dolores Huerta y César Chávez by Monica Brown, illustrated by Joe Cepeda
Harvesting Hope: The Story of Cesar Chavez by Kathleen Krull, illustrated by Yuyi Morales
Who Was Cesar Chavez? by Dana Meachen Rau
Dolores Huerta: A Hero to Migrant Workers by Sarah Warren, illustrated by Robert Casilla

Author's Note

Some of my fondest memories from childhood are of cooking with the women in my family. It is the foundation for all I have spent my life working on. Today, I love sharing my passion for cooking with my daughter, Krishna. Our most treasured times together are spent shopping for ingredients at the farmers market and running home to cook our bounty for the evening's meal. Nothing brings us closer than food. It helps me connect her to our culture. It's a time for stories and family history. And I use these cooking activities to teach Krishna not only how to cook but *what* to cook and *when*. A child who cooks her own food is more likely to eat it. And to eat *well*. Children feel a proprietorship and pride in what they've cooked (even when it's "healthy" for them!). Teaching children how to cook gives them the gift of good eating *long* after we are gone. The pleasure that comes from making something with my child, and then savoring it together, is magical.

I believe that being able to feed ourselves well at home using simple ingredients is the healthiest thing we can do for our family in the long run. My hope is that you will use the recipes in this book to bring your family together in health and happiness.

For Krishna, who gives meaning to everything. —P.L.

For those who feed us,
especially the farmworkers all around the world. —J.M.N.

VIKING

An imprint of Penguin Random House LLC, New York

First published in the United States of America by Viking, an imprint of Penguin Random House LLC, 2021

Visit us online at penguinrandomhouse.com.

Library of Congress Cataloging-in-Publication Data is available.

Manufactured in China

ISBN 9780593202708

10 9 8 7 6 5 4 3 2 1

RRD
Design by Kate Renner   Text set in Palatino Sans

The art for this picture book was created using acrylic paints and colored pencils on hand-textured paper.